Where Is My Home?

Terry Treetop Series

Tali Carmi

Where is My Home?

Terry Treetop Series

Written by Tali Carmi

TALI CARMI
kids' books & more

Where Is My Home Copyright © 2013 by Tali Carmi

Forth edition - 03/2017

Contact Tali Carmi:

Website: www.thekidsbooks.com

Twitter: tbcarmi

Facebook: Tali.Carmi.Author

LinkedIn: Tali Carmi

Join mailing list: www.thekidsbooks.com/join-mailing-list

mail: tcarmi@naharsite.com

ISBN: 978-1495200007

To Nave, Hofit, Rimon and Benny

Thank you for making my home what it is!

Terry loved climbing trees, so much that everyone called him Terry Treetop.

It was summer vacation, and for Terry, this was the best time of the year!

He sat in his favorite place in the whole wide world, his tree house, dreaming of all the adventures he would have this summer.

As Terry daydreamed, he watched a butterfly land to rest on a flower nearby.

"Hello! What are you doing there?" Terry waved. The butterfly didn't answer.

Terry rushed down from his tree house, curious to see the pretty butterfly up close.

The butterfly paid no mind as Terry tried to gain its attention.

It kept flying from one flower to the next, beyond the trees and across the stream, while Terry chased after it. "Please, stop! I just want to meet you!" But, the butterfly didn't listen.

After what felt like ages, Terry finally stopped to catch his breath. When he looked up again, the pretty butterfly had gone. Sad and hungry, he decided to go home.

But as Terry turned around, he realized something very scary...

He had no idea where he was!

As Terry looked around, feeling very confused, he noticed a little rabbit hopping by. "Hello!" Terry exclaimed, "My name is Terry. I'm hungry, and I can't find my way home. Can you please help me?" The rabbit smiled. "Sure, Terry! I'm Robby. You can come to my house. We have lots of food!"

And Terry was off on another journey with his new friend, Robby.

Robby lived in a little burrow between the bushes and the high grass, with his mom, dad, brothers and sisters. As they arrived, the new friends discovered that Terry was much too big for the burrow. He couldn't get inside, no matter how hard he tried!

Fortunately, Robby's mom had an idea. "Don't worry, Terry! You just sit right here, and I'll bring you some of Robby's favorite food, fresh clover!"

Terry was excited to try it, but as he bit into the little plant, he realized it wasn't tasty at all. "Thank you for being so kind. Can you tell me how to get home?" Terry asked Robby's mom. "Just go past the tall grass and reach the stream. Your home is just behind it."

Terry did as she told him, and reached the stream. Terry walked over to find a beaver, enjoying the water. "Hello!" Terry waved. "My name is Terry. I'm on my way home, but I'm very hungry. Do you know where I can find some food?"

"Hello! I'm Bono. Why don't you come with me? We have lots of food!"
Terry excitedly followed Bono as his stomach began to rumble.

Bono's lodge was on the other side of the stream. It was big and sturdy.

"I live here with my mom, dad and four brothers." Bono said. "It's safe and comfy, and we can swim into our home, because the door is under water!"

Terry was grateful, but he wasn't a very good swimmer.

"You don't have to come in. I'll bring you one of my favorite foods, a water lily!" Terry tried it but, like the clover, it didn't taste very good.

So he thankfully said goodbye and continued across the stream.

It was already noon, and Terry knew that his mom would be calling him for lunch soon. As Terry walked along, he came across a fawn eating the fresh, green grass.

"Hello! My name is Terry," he introduced himself. "I'm hungry and still a long way from home. Do you know where I can find some food?" His stomach was roaring.

"Hello!" The fawn replied. "I'm Freddy! You can try some of this grass here. It's yummy!" Freddy's mom joined them, curious to see who her son was talking to. She was always keeping a very close eye on him. Terry thought of his own mom and how she did the same thing. He missed her very much.

"Hello, little boy," Freddy's mom greeted Terry. "You look lost."

"I miss my mom," Terry answered sadly.

"I'm sure she is waiting for you," Freddy's mom replied softly. "Just go to the end of this meadow and continue straight. There, you will find your home." Terry thanked her and headed home!

When he crossed the meadow, he reached a grove where he met a squirrel.

"Hello! My name is Terry. I'm looking for my home. I was told it would be on the other side of the meadow, but, this is your grove, not my home. I'm so lost, and very hungry."

"Hi, Terry. I'm Suzanne. I'm sorry. I don't know where you live. But, I have some food to share!"

Terry climbed eagerly up the tree after Suzanne. His name was Terry Treetop, after all. He followed Suzanne all the way to her nest at the top of the tree, but it was too small for Terry to fit inside. "Don't worry!" Suzanne told him. "Just stay here! I'll bring you some food!" And she brought him three nuts and one big acorn.

Terry was about to try this new food, when something wonderful happened! From the top of Suzanne's tree, he could see his very own tree house!

"I can see my tree house!" He cried with joy. He hugged Suzanne and scurried down the tree. "Thank you! Now, I must be off!" And, he rushed towards his tree house.

When Terry finally reached his home, he was so happy! Everything was the right size. Inside, his mom was waiting for him, and his favorite food, apple pie, was on the table. "It's very nice making new friends and trying new things, but there's no place like home!" Terry said joyfully.

As he was about to go inside, he saw the pretty butterfly land on a flower in his mom's yard. Terry smiled, "Oh, no! I won't chase you again! It's time to go home, Goodbye!" Terry waved to the butterfly and went inside.

Thank you!

This book has been created with love and joy

And it is very important for me to hear

what you think about it.

Please press the link below and leave a review.

Your thoughts mean a lot to me.

Lot's of Love
- Tali